RAYMOND CHANDLER'S

MARLOWE

Graphic novel

ibooks
graphic novels

DISTRIBUTED BY SIMON & SCHUSTER

Ibooks, inc.
24 West 25th Street
New York, NY 10010

The ibooks world wide web site address is: http://www.ibooks.net

Interior design by Dean Motter
Additional design by Jeof Vita, J. Vita and Les Munoz

ISBN: 0-7434-7489-9

10 9 8 7 6 5 4 3 2 1

Series Editor: Byron Preiss
Consulting Editor: Howard Zimmerman
Editor: Dean Motter

Share your thoughts about *Raymond Chandler's Marlowe* and other ibooks graphic novels on the ibooks virtual reading group at www.ibooks.net

GOLDFISH

Adapted by
TOM DeHAVEN

Illustrated by
RIAN HUGHES

Lettered by
WILLIE SCHUBERT

ALL RIGHT, I KNOW IT SOUNDS SCREWY. ALL THOSE YEARS GONE BY AND THE SMART GUYS THAT MUST HAVE WORKED ON THE CASE--AND THEN A COKEHEAD TURNS IT UP.

BUT HE'S A NICE LITTLE RUNT, MARLOWE, AND SOMEHOW I BELIEVE HIM.

HE KNOWS WHERE SYPE IS. AND HE WANTS HELP TO COLLECT.

SO WHERE IS SYPE?

THAT'S THE ONLY THING HE WON'T TELL ME-- THAT AND THE NAME SYPE IS USING NOW. BUT IT'S SOMEWHERE UP NORTH, IN OR NEAR OLYMPIA, WASHINGTON. PEELER SAW HIM UP THERE.

HE'S LIVING UP THERE WITH HIS WIFE. HIS WIFE AND HIS GOLDFISH.

GOLDFISH?

YEAH. SYPE JUST PLAYS AROUND WITH GOLDFISH. HIS HOBBY, I GUESS.

SO WILL YOU GO SEE PEELER? IF I GIVE YOU THE KEY, WILL YOU GO TALK TO HIM--

--BEFORE HE GETS JUNKED UP FOR THE EVENING?

SURE, KATHY. IF THAT'S WHAT YOU WANT.

I DON'T RATE MUCH IN IT. MAYBE NOT ANYTHING. BUT IF I COULD HAVE A GRAND OR TWO WAITING FOR JOHNNY WHEN HE CAME OUT, MAYBE...

IT'S A DREAM, KATHY, IT'S ALL A DREAM.

BUT IF IT ISN'T, YOU CAN HAVE AN EVEN THIRD.

She'd never reform that little crook she'd married. But she'd nev give up trying, either. Maybe that's how com I liked her.

The last time I had been in the Gray Lake district I had helped a D.A.'s man named Bernie Ohls shoot a gunman named Poke Andrews. But that was higher up the hill...

I rang Peeler's bell, but nobody answered. So I let myself into Kathy's apartment...

...and got into his place through a connecting door.

MARDO? PEELER MARDO?

"SO DID YOU SEE HIM, MARLOWE?"

When I'd gone over to see Peeler, frankly I'd thought it was all hooey. Now I wasn't so sure. If he'd opened up to his killers, we were through, and so was Sype. Unless I could find him first.

The Reliance Indemnity company had offices in the Graas Building, three small rooms that looked like nothing at all. They were a big enough outfit to be as shabby as they liked.

The resident manager was named Lutin.

MARLOWE, EH? I'VE HEARD OF YOU. WHAT'S ON YOU MIND?

REMEMBER THE LEANDER PEARLS?

I'M NOT LIKELY TO FORGET THEM. THEY COST THIS COMPANY A HUNDRED AND FIFTY THOUSAND DOLLARS. I WAS A COCKY YOUNG ADJUSTER THEN.

I'VE GOT AN IDEA. IT MAY BE ALL HAYWIRE, BUT I WANT TO TRY IT OUT.

IS YOUR TWENTY-FIVE-GRAND REWARD STILL GOOD?

YOU'RE WASTING YOUR TIME, MARLOWE.

EXCUSE ME.

THOSE MARBLES EXISTED, DIDN'T THEY?

DARN RIGHT THEY EXISTED.

AND IF THEY STILL DO, THEY BELONG TO US. BUT SYPE NEVER HAD THOSE PEARLS. IF HE HAD, HE'D HAVE MADE SOME KIND OF TERMS WITH US YEARS AGO.

LISTEN, I KNOW YOU'RE CRAZY, BUT IF YOU DO GET ANYTHING, BRING IT IN THROUGH OUR BOYS. WE NEED THE ADVERTISING.

AN THE TWENTY-FIVE GRAND?

STILL STANDS, MARLOWE.

It was a quarter to five when I got back to the office. I had a couple of short drinks, and a pipe and was sitting down to interview my brains when the phone rang.

MARLOWE?

A woman's voice. Small, tight, and cold. I didn't know it.

BETTER SEE RUSH MADDER. KNOW HIM?

NO. WHY SHOULD I SEE HIM?

ON ACCOUNT OF A GUY HAD SORE FEET.

CLIK!

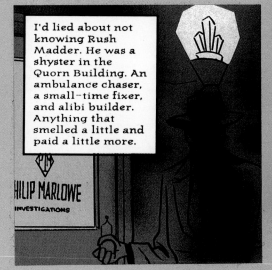

I'd lied about not knowing Rush Madder. He was a shyster in the Quorn Building. An ambulance chaser, a small-time fixer, and alibi builder. Anything that smelled a little and paid a little more.

But I hadn't heard of him in connection with any big operations. Like burning people's feet.

--ACHE ME SHOOT--MMM--LOWE.

--'P IT OFF. YOU'RE THROUGH.

DON'T BE A GOOF. A FEW HOURS' SLEEP FOR YOU, A FEW HOURS' START FOR US. I MEAN IT, MARLOWE, DON'T MAKE ME SHOOT. BECAUSE I WOULD.

Carol Donovan. I presumed.

TWO-WAY SPLIT, EH? HE DOESN'T LIKE MY METHOD, EH? BLESS HIS BIG SOFT HEART. WE'LL SEE ABOUT H--

Then the floor rose up and bumped me.

As I floated off, I felt a dull jar that might've been a shot. I hoped she had shot Madden. No such luck. She'd merely helped me on my way out—with my own sap.

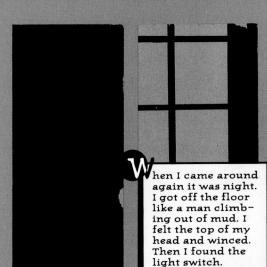

KATHY? IT'S MARLOWE, YOU ALONE?

When I came around again it was night. I got off the floor like a man climbing out of mud. I felt the top of my head and winced. Then I found the light switch.

YES, BUT I HAVEN'T BEEN. THE HOUSE HAS BEEN FULL OF COPPERS FOR HOURS. OLD GRUDGE OF SOME KIND, THEY FIGURE. JUST LIKE YOU SAID THEY WOULD.

BUT I'M GLAD YOU CALLED, PHIL. I WAS AFRAID YOU'D BE GONE ALREADY.

AND WHERE WAS I SUPPOSED TO BE GOING?

WELL...YOU KNOW. YOUR GIRL TOLD ME. CAROL DONOVAN. SHE HAD YOUR CARD. WHY, WASN'T IT...?

I DON'T HAVE ANY GIRL.

AND I BET A NAME SLIPPED PAST YOUR LIPS--THE NAME OF A TOWN UP NORTH. DID IT?

As soon as she said yes, I hung up.

I had a sore head and a raging thirst and what I wanted most was a brandy, sitting by myself in a quiet little bar.

Instead, I caught the night plane north.

GOLD SHOP

Olympia, Washington.

In the morning, I took a room at the Snoqualmie Hotel, then walked down a hill to the last, loneliest reach of Puget Sound.

NICE AND QUIET HERE-- RESTFUL. I LIKE A TOWN LIKE THIS.

A MAN THAT'S BEEN AROUND A TOWN LIKE THIS KNOWS EVERYBODY IN IT, I BET.

YOU'D LOSE.

KNOW ANYBODY AROUND HERE THAT KEEPS A LOT OF GOLDFISH?

I put my dollar in my pocket and went back up the hill. I figured it would take too long to learn his language.

Capitol Way ran north and south. I walked north.

Occasionally I'd stop in some-where, ask about goldfish.

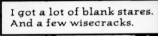

I got a lot of blank stares. And a few wisecracks.

DO I LOOK LIKE A GUY WHO WOULD KNOW A GUY WHO WOULD HAVE GOLDFISH?

SO HOW'S PEELER?

HITTING IT HIGH, AS USUAL.

NAME'S MARLOWE. I DIDN'T CATCH YOURS.

CALL ME SUNSET. I'M ALWAYS MOVING WEST.

GOT A ROOM SOME-WHERE?

HOTEL.

LET'S HANG, MARLOWE.

On the walk back down Capitol Way, Sunset kept looking over at me—a little at a time, but very thoroughly.

LISTEN, I DON'T KNOW YOU FROM LAST SUNDAY'S SPORTS SECTION. YOU MAY BE ALL TO THE SILK. I JUST DON'T KNOW.

SO WHY'D YOU BRACE ME?

YOU HAD THE PASSWORD, DIDN'T YOU?

YEAH. GOLDFISH WAS THE PASSWORD. THE SMOKE SHOP WAS THE PLACE.

It was one of those breaks you dream of, but don't handle right—even in dreams.

WHAT'S SO FUNNY, MARLOWE?

NOTHING. ABSOLUTELY NOTHING. HOW ABOUT WE GO HAVE A DRINK?

So we went up to my room and sat down and studied each other over a couple of glasses of scotch and ice water. The two of us were pretty cagey characters, all right. But it wasn't getting us anywhere.

WE COULD GO ON LIKE THIS FOR WEEKS. SO LET'S PUT OUR CARDS THE TABLE. WHERE'S THE OLD GUY?

YOU MEAN WHY DON'T I PUT MY CARDS ON THE TABLE AND YOU JUST SIT BACK AND LOOK 'EM OVER.

NIX.

THEN HOW DO YOU LIKE THIS? PEELER'S DEAD.

THERE'S SOME COMPETITION YOU TWO BIRDS DIDN'T KNOW ABOUT.

Madder made a sudden whimper, then his eyes turned up in his head and he fell forward in a dead faint.

But Sunset was mistaken.

IF YOU'RE GOING TO SHOOT ME, DO IT NOW, SHAMUS.

YOU WON'T GET A SECOND CHANCE.

ENOUGH EXERCISE? DON'T GET UP!

LISTEN A MINUTE, MARLOWE--

--IT'S JUST YOU AND ME NOW. TWO-WAY SPLIT. COME ON, WHAT DO YOU SAY? DEAL?

I NEVER DEAL WITH SAVAGE LITTLE BRATS.

It was all right with me if she wanted to jump out the window. It was a long drop to the payement.

Madder was still out cold—and there was nothing I could do for Sunset.

I needed a car to get out to Westport. But that was no big problem. Thanks to Miss Donovan.

It took about ten minutes to find where they'd parked their car...

...then I was on my way—heading toward the Pacific Ocean.

And Wally Sype.

An hour's fast driving punctuated by the cough of a head gasket brought me within the sound of surf.

WESTPORT 9ᴹ

Twenty minutes later I chugged into Westport—the farthest west a man could go and still be on the mainland of the United States.

A swell place for an ex-convict to hide out with a couple of somebody else's pearls...

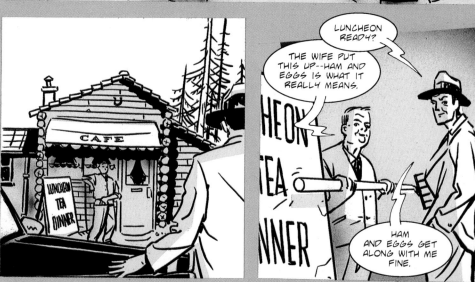

CAFE

LUNCHEON
TEA
DINNER

LUNCHEON READY?

THE WIFE PUT THIS UP--HAM AND EGGS IS WHAT IT REALLY MEANS.

HAM AND EGGS GET ALONG WITH ME FINE.

THE MISSUS SAYS YOU MUST BE TALKING ABOUT OLD WALLACE. WE DON'T KNOW HIM RIGHT WELL.

HE DON'T ACT NEIGHBORLY.

YEAH, I GUESS THAT'S YOUR GOLDFISH MAN, ALL RIGHT. OLD WALLACE. LIVES UP TOP OF THAT HILL THERE. THE PINK HOUSE.

NAME'S WALLACE, EH?

UH-HUH. IT'S JUST HIM AND HIS WIFE UP THERE.

That ended my interest in ham and eggs.

There didn't seem to be any hurry now. I knew where Sype was—and Carol Donovan didn't.

Rush Madder would come out of his faint and turn the girl loose.

But they didn't know anything about Westport.

Sunset hadn't mentioned the place in their presence.

So I had time.

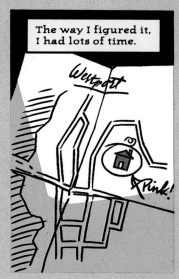

The way I figured it, I had lots of time.

Westport

So I took a long walk around the town before running up to Sype's place.

There didn't seem to be any law enforcement around.

Late in the afternoon, I decided to go get it over with—and meet the man who'd stolen the Leander pearls.

WHITE FUNGUS. IT AIN'T SO BAD. I'LL TRIM THE FELLER UP AND HE'LL BE RIGHT AS RAIN.

WHAT CAN I DO FOR YOU, MISTER?

I GUESS FISH GET THINGS WRONG WITH THEM, TOO-- LIKE PEOPLE.

YEAH. SOME YOU CAN CURE AND SOME YOU CAN'T.

THIS DON'T HURT HIM, CASE YOU THINK IT DOES. YOU CAN SHOCK A FISH TO DEATH BUT YOU CAN'T HURT IT LIKE A PERSON.

INTERESTED IN FISH, ARE YOU?

NOT ESPECIALLY. THAT WAS JUST AN EXCUSE.

I CAME A LONG WAY TO SEE YOU, MR. SYPE.

BLAM!

CRASSSHH!

It was very still in the room for a little while. I heard the surf booming in the distance. Then I heard a whistling sound close at hand.

It was Sype, trying to say something.

THE MOORS, HATTIE-- THE MOORS.

I like goldfish as well as the next man, but business is business and crime is crime. I found a razor blade and went to work.

It was a messy job, but it took only about five minutes.

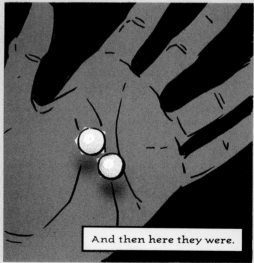

And then here they were.

THE PENCIL

Adapted by
JEROME CHARYN

Drawn by
DAVID LLOYD

Lettered by
ELITTA FELL

I HEARD YOU LEVELED WITH THE CUSTOMERS, MARLOWE.

THAT'S WHY I STAY POOR.

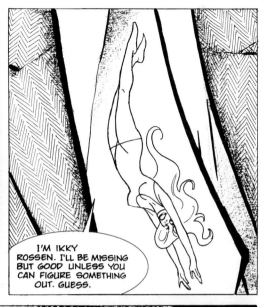

I'M IKKY ROSSEN. I'LL BE MISSING BUT GOOD UNLESS YOU CAN FIGURE SOMETHING OUT. GUESS.

I'VE ALREADY GUESSED. YOU TELL ME AND TELL ME QUICK. I DON'T HAVE ALL NIGHT TO WATCH YOU FEEDING ME WITH AN EYE-DROPPER.

I RAN OUT ON THE OUTFIT. THE HIGH BOYS DON'T LIKE THAT... I DONE BAD THINGS.

I SCARED AND HURT GUYS. I NEVER KILLED NOBODY. THAT'S NOTHING TO THE OUTFIT. THEY PICK UP A PENCIL AND THEY DRAW A LINE. I GOT THE WORD. THEIR OPERATORS ARE ON THE WAY... AND THEY KNOW WHERE I LIVE.

NO GOOD NOW. I'M COVERED.

A THOUSAND NOW... AND YOU GOT FIVE COMING IF YOU PRY ME LOOSE.

SUPPOSE -- JUST SUPPOSE -- I COULD FIGURE AN OUT FOR YOU. WHAT'S YOUR NEXT MOVE?

I KNOW A PLACE -- IF I COULD GET THERE WITHOUT BEING TAILED ... A GOOD-SIZED PLACE, BUT STILL PRETTY CLEAN.

I NEED A HELPER. I KNOW A GIRL. DAUGHTER OF A CHIEF OF POLICE WHO GOT BROKEN FOR HONESTY.

YOU GOT NO RIGHT TO RISK HER. WOMEN AIN'T BUILT FOR THE ROUGH STUFF.

THERE WON'T BE ANY ROUGH STUFF IF I'M LUCKY...

ANNE, I NEED YOUR HELP.

THE ONLY T EVER SE

I'VE GOT A CLIENT WHO IS AN EX-HOOD, USED TO BE A TROUBLESHOOTER FOR THE OUTFIT, THE SYNDICATE, THE BIG MOB... STOP MOVING YOUR LEGS AROUND. OR PUT ON A PAIR OF SLACKS.

MARLOWE, CAN'T YOU THINK OF ANYTHING ELSE?

HIS NAME IS IKKY ROSSEN. HE'S NOT BEAUTIFUL AND HE'S NOT ANYTHING I LIKE — EXCEPT ONE THING, HE GOT MAD WHEN I SAID I NEEDED A GIRL HELPER.

HE SAID WOMEN WEREN'T MADE FOR THE ROUGH STUFF. THAT'S WHY I TOOK THE JOB. TO A REAL MOBSTER, A WOMAN MEANS NO MORE THAN A SACK OF FLOUR.

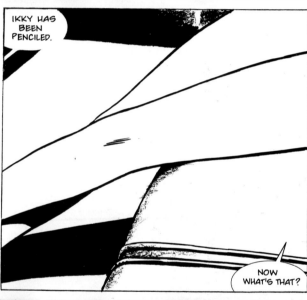

IKKY HAS BEEN PENCILED.

NOW WHAT'S THAT?

YOU HAVE A LIST. YOU DRAW A LINE THROUGH A NAME WITH A PENCIL. THE GUY IS AS GOOD AS DEAD.

MARLOWE, AT LEAST YOU COULD TAKE OFF YOUR HAT.

YOU CAN HELP ME SPOT THE PLANE AND SEE WHERE THEY GO - THE OPERATORS ASSIGNED TO THE JOB.

IT'S MY GUESS THEY'LL BE ARRIVING FROM NEW YORK TOMORROW MORNING...YOU KNOW WHAT THEY LOOK LIKE?

OH, SURE. I MEET KILLERS EVERY DAY.

THEY'LL LOOK LIKE ANYONE WHO'S IN A QUIET WELL-RUN BUSINESS OR PROFESSION. THEY'LL HAVE QUIET CLOTHES AND THEY'LL BE POLITE — WHEN THEY WANT TO BE. THEY'LL HAVE BRIEF-CASES WITH GUNS IN THEM THAT HAVE CHANGED HANDS SO OFTEN THEY CAN'T POSSIBLY BE TRACED...

THEY'LL GO TO A HOTEL FIRST, BUT THEY HAVE IKKY'S ADDRESS. THEY'LL MOVE INTO SOME PLACE WHERE THEY CAN WATCH IKKY UP CLOSE.

WILL THEY SHOOT HIM FROM A ROOM OR APARTMENT ACROSS THE STREET?

NO. THEY'LL SHOOT HIM FROM THREE FEET AWAY. THEY'LL WALK UP BEHIND HIM AND SAY 'HELLO, IKKY'.

I NEED A DRINK.

YOU'RE THE DAMNDEST GUY. WOMEN DO ANYTHING YOU WANT THEM TO. HOW COME I'M STILL A VIRGIN AT TWENTY-EIGHT?

WHY DON'T YOU GET MARRIED?

I DON'T KNOW ANY REALLY NICE MEN — EXCEPT YOU.

I WAS WORRIED, ANNE.

I COULDN'T GET THEIR NAMES. CLERKS DON'T LEAVE REGISTRATION CARDS LYING AROUND THESE DAYS. BUT I RODE UP IN THE ELEVATOR WITH THEM AND SPOTTED THEIR ROOM...

WHAT WERE THEY LIKE?

THEIR EYES WERE INTERESTING, VERY QUICK TO MOVE, VERY OBSERVANT, WATCHING EVERYTHING NEAR THEM... IT'S A GOOD THING I DISCOVERED THEM AND NOT YOU. YOU DON'T LOOK LIKE A COP, BUT YOU DON'T LOOK LIKE A MAN WHO IS NOT A COP. YOU HAVE MARKS ON YOU.

MARLOWE, DO I GET A DINNER AND MAYBE A KISS?

IF THEY'RE THE RIGHT MEN, THEY'LL FOLLOW ME. I ALREADY TOOK AN APARTMENT ACROSS FROM IKKY — A BLOCK ON POYNTER WITH SIX LOW-LIFE APARTMENT HOUSES... SO LONG, ANNE. SEE YOU.

WHEN YOU NEED HELP.

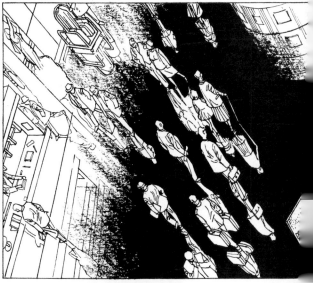

AR
YOU PH
MARLO

WHAT CAN I DO FOR YOU?

YOU CAN LAY OFF IKKY ROSSEN, OR YOU CAN GET YOUR BELLY FULL OF LEAD.

WHAT MAKES YOU THINK I KNOW ANY IKKY ROSSEN?

LET'S GO INTO
THINKING PAR

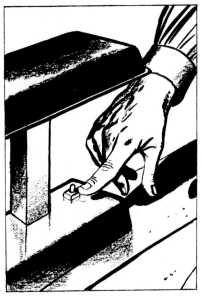

I'D LIKE TO TALK TO BERNIE OHLS... BERNIE, THIS IS MARLOWE. WE HAVEN'T HAD A FIGHT IN YEARS. I'M GETTING LONELY.

WELL, GET MARRIED. I'M CHIEF INVESTIGATOR FOR THE SHERIFF'S OFFICE NOW. I DON'T HARDLY SPEAK TO PRIVATE EYES.

SPEAK TO THIS ONE. I NEED HELP. I'M ON A TICKLISH JOB WHERE I COULD GET KILLED ... IF I CALL YOU, COME RUNNING OR SEND A COUPLE OF GOOD BOYS.

IKKY, BE READY TO MOVE OUT ABOUT MIDNIGHT. WE'VE SPOTTED YOUR BOYFRIENDS AND THEY'RE HOLED UP AT A HOTEL IN BEVERLY HILLS...

...YOU'VE BEEN CARELESS, IKKY. YOU WERE FOLLOWED TO MY OFFICE. THAT CUT THE TIME WE HAVE.

WHERE'S THE BACK DOOR OF YOUR FLOP?

IN BACK. WHERE WOULD IT BE? IN THE ALLEY.

LEAVE YOUR SUIT-CASE THERE. WE WALK OUT TOGETHER. AND GO TO YOUR CAR. WE DRIVE BY THE ALLEY AND PICK UP THE SUITCASE...

SUPPOSE SOME GU STEALS IT?

YEAH, SUPPOSE YOU GET DEAD. WHICH DO YOU LIKE BETTER?

I'M SCARED.

ME TOO, IF IT HELPS ANY.

WHEN WE GET OUT-
SIDE, KEEP BOTH HANDS
IN YOUR COAT POCKETS
AND THE GUN IN YOUR
RIGHT HAND...

IF
ANYBODY CALLS
OUT YOUR NAME
BEHIND YOU, TURN
FAST AND SHOOT.

LAUNDRY

I'LL GET
YOUR SUIT-
CASE.

cigarette
should!

THIS IS FAR ENOUGH FOR ME, IKKY. I'LL GRAB A BUS BACK IF THERE IS ONE...

FIVE GRAND, LIKE I PROMISED.

I DON'T REALLY FEEL I EARNED ALL TH IT WAS TOO EA

TAKE THE DOUGH. I GOT PLENTY. YOU DID WHAT I ASKED... YOUR TROUBLES ARE JUST BEGINNING. THE OUTFIT HAS EYES AND EARS EVERYWHERE.

YOU WORK LATE, MR. MARLOWE. BUT YOU ALWAYS DID, DIDN'T YOU?

IT'S THAT SORT OF BUSINESS ...THANKS, JIMMY.

MARLOWE, I KNOW YOU CAN'T WAIT TO SEE ME... BUT NOT IN THE MIDDLE OF THE NIGHT.

ANNE, DON'T MOVE AROUND MUCH... I GOT A PENCIL IN THE MAIL.

OH, THE OUTFIT'S LITT CALLING CARD YOU'D BETTE COME OVER HE AND HIDE

NO, THAT WOULD ONLY DRAW THE BULLY BOYS TO YOU... IT'S A WARNING, ANNE, A POLITE SLAP IN THE FACE. THE SYNDICATE IS SAYING, "WHEN WE PENCIL A GUY, ANY GUY THAT TRIES TO HELP HIM IS IN FOR A SMASHING."

MARLOWE, WHERE WILL YOU GO?

NOT TO MY PLACE. I GO TO THE POYNTER STR APARTMENT. TH THE SAFEST

CALL ME, MARLOWE... AS SOON AS YOU CAN. I'LL BE WAITING HERE FOR YOU.

LOOK, SWEETNESS, DON'T BE SO GENEROUS. SAVE THE CRUMBS FOR A RAINY DAY. ALL I WANT IS TWO EGGS THREE MINUTES --NO MORE-- A SLICE OF YOUR CONCRETE TOAST, A BIG HAPPY SMILE, AND DON'T GIVE ANYBODY ELSE ANY COFFEE. I MIGHT NEED IT ALL.

I GOT A COLD. DON'T PUSH ME AROUND. I MIGHT CRACK YOU ONE ON THE KISSER.

LET'S BE PALS. I HAD A ROUGH NIGHT TOO.

HEY, IKKY!

SO LONG,
IKKY.

IT'S MARLOWE, I'M IN TROUBLE-- REAL TROUBLE.

WHY TELL ME? YOU MUST BE USED TO IT BY NOW.

THIS KIND OF TROUBLE YOU DON'T GET USED TO. I'D LIKE TO COME OVER AND TELL YOU ABOUT IT.

YOU IN THE SAME OFFICE?

THE SAME.

...AVE TO GO ...AT WAY, I'LL DROP IN.

EVER HEAR OF A CHARACTER NAMED IKKY ROSSEN?...AN EX-MOBSTER WHO GOT DISLIKED BY THE MOB. THEY PUT A PENCIL THROUGH HIS NAME AND SENT THE USUAL TWO TOUGH GUYS ON A PLANE. HE GOT TIPPED AND HIRED ME TO HELP HIM GET AWAY.

NICE CLEAN WORK.

CUT IT OUT, BERNIE. A GIRL I KNOW SPOTTED THE BOYS AND TAILED THEM TO A HOTEL. THIS GIRL—

WOULD SHE HAVE A NAME?

ONLY FOR YOU. HER NAME IS ANNE RIORDAN. SHE LIVES IN BAY CITY. HER FATHER WAS ONCE CHIEF OF POLICE THERE...

I TOOK AN APARTMENT OPPOSITE IKKY. THE BAD BOYS WERE STILL AT THE HOTEL... I GOT IKKY OUT AND DROVE HIM AS FAR AS POMONA AND I MOVED INTO THE APARTMENT ON POYNTER STREET, RIGHT ACROSS FROM HIS DUMP.

WHY -- IF HE WAS ALREADY GONE?

BECAUSE SOMEONE S ME THIS

THEY KNEW YOU WERE IN ON IT?

IKKY WAS TAILED HERE BY A LITTLE SQUIRT WHO LATER CAME AROUND AND STUCK A GUN IN MY STOMACH. I KNOCKED HIM AROUND A BIT, BUT I HAD TO LET HIM GO. I THOUGHT POYNTER STREET WAS SAFER AFTER THAT. I LIVE LONELY.

I GET AROUND. I HEAR REPORTS. SO THEY GUNNED THE WRONG GUY.

SAME HEIGHT, SAME BUILD, SAME GENERAL APPEARANCE. I SAW THEM GUN HIM...TWO GUYS IN DARK SUITS WITH HATS PULLED DOWN.

I DON'T THINK THEY'LL BOTHER WITH YOU NOW. THEY'VE HIT THE WRONG GUY. THE MOB WILL BE VERY QUIET FOR A WHILE...

I'LL TALK TO THE CITY HOMICIDE BOYS. I DON'T GUESS YOU'RE IN ANY TROUBLE. BUT YOU SAW THE SHOOTING. THEY'LL WANT TO TALK TO YOU, PHIL. THEY JUST LOVE THEIR TAPE RECORDERS.

I DON'T LIKE THE PENCIL. AND I DON'T LIKE THE WRONG MAN BEING KILLED —PROBABLY SOME POOR BOOKKEEPER IN A CHEAP BUSINESS OR HE WOULDN'T BE LIVING IN THAT NEIGHBORHOOD.

YOU SHOULD NEVER HAVE TOUCHED IT, PHIL.

MR. PHILIP MARLOWE? I'M FOSTER GRIMES FROM LAS VEGAS. I RUN THE RANCHO ESPERANZA ON SOUTH FIFTH. I HEAR YOU GOT INVOLVED WITH A MAN NAMED IKKY ROSSEN.

WHERE IS IKKY NOW, IF YOU KNOW?

I DON'T KNOW. I HELPED HIM LEAVE TOWN. I'M TELLING YOU THIS, ALTHOUGH I DON'T KNOW WHO THE HELL YOU ARE, BECAUSE I'VE ALREADY TOLD AN OLD FRIEND-ENEMY OF MINE, A TOP MAN WITH THE SHERIFF'S OFFICE.

WHAT'S A FRIEND-ENEMY?

LAWMEN DON'T GO AROUND KISSING ME, BUT I'VE KNOWN HIM FOR YEARS.

I HAVE A UNIQUE SETUP IN VEGAS. WE OWN THE PLACE EXCEPT FOR ONE LOUSY NEWSPAPER EDITOR...

...WE LET HIM LIVE BECAUSE LETTING HIM LIVE MAKES US LOOK BETTER THAN KNOCKING HIM OFF. KILLINGS ARE NOT GOOD BUSINESS ANYMORE.

LIKE IKKY ROSSEN.

THAT'S NOT A KILLING. IT'S AN EXECUTION. IKKY GOT OUT OF LINE.

SO YOUR GI... BOYS HAD T... RUB THE WRO... GUY.

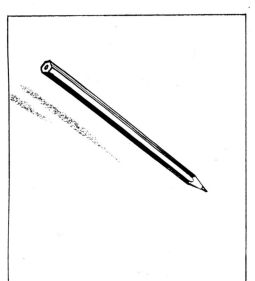

IT CAME BY SPECIAL DELIVERY. NO MESSAGE, NO RETURN ADDRESS. JUST THE PENCIL. THINK I'VE NEVER HEARD ABOUT THE PENCIL, MR. GRIMES?

LOOK UNDER THE DESK, MR. GRIMES. YOU'LL SEE A .45. IT'S POINTING AT YOUR BELLY.

NICE WORK, MARLOWE. WE COULD USE A MAN LIKE YOU...

TELL ME SOMETHING, MR. GRIMES. WHY PICK ON ME? APART FROM IKKY, WHAT DID I EVER DO TO MAKE YOU DISLIKE ME?

THE LARSEN CASE. YOU HELPED SEND ONE OF OUR BOYS TO THE GAS CHAMBER.

THAT WE DON'T FORGET. WE HAD YOU IN MIND AS A FALL GUY FOR IKKY. YOU'LL ALWAYS BE A FALL GUY... SOMETHING WILL HIT YOU WHEN YOU LEAST EXPECT IT.

WHO LET YOU IN HERE?

DID YOU FORGET? MY FATHER WAS A POLICE CHIEF... I COULD ALWAYS PICK A LOCK.

I'M GOING TO LOOK FOR IKKY. I HAVE TO. IF I DON'T CALL YOU IN THREE DAYS, GET HOLD OF BERNIE OHLS. I'M GOING TO FLAGSTAFF, ARIZONA. IKKY SAYS HE'LL BE THERE.

YOU'RE A FOOL. IT'S SOME SORT OF A TRAP.

A MR. GRIMES OF VEGAS VISITED ME WITH A SILENCED GUN... IF I FIND IKKY AND REPORT TO GRIMES, THE MOB WILL LET ME ALONE.

YOU'D CONDEMN A MAN TO DEATH?

IKKY WON'T BE THERE WHEN I REPORT. HE'LL BE ON A PLANE TO EUROPE WITH FORGED PAPERS. BUT THE OUTFIT HAS LONG ARMS AND IKKY WON'T HAVE A DULL LIFE STAYING ALIVE. HE HASN'T ANY CHOICE. FOR HIM IT'S EITHER HIDE OR GET THE PENCIL.

SO CLEVER OF YOU, DARLING. WHAT ABOUT YOUR OWN PENCIL?

IT'S JUST A BIT OF SCARE TECHNIQUE.

AND YOU DON'T SCARE, YOU WONDERFUL HANDSOME BRUTE.

I SCARE. BUT DOESN'T PARALY ME.

WHAT GIVES?

YOU READ THE PAPERS?

JUST THE SPORTS SECTION.

LET'S GO TO YOUR ROOM AND TALK ABOUT IT.

THE TWO OPERATORS GOT UP TOO EARLY... THEY SHOT A GUY WHO LOOKED A LITTLE LIKE YOU.

THAT'S A HOT ONE. BUT THE OUTFIT WILL FIND OUT. SO THE TAG FOR ME STAYS ON.

YOU MUST THINK I'M DUMB

BUT I BEGAN TO SEE THE FLAW. WHY WOULD YOU LET A LITTLE PUNK LIKE THAT CHARLES HICKON TRAIL YOU TO MY OFFICE?

SOME POOR JERK FROM THE EAST GETS INVOLVED WITH THE MOB. HE TRIES TO BREAK LOOSE. HE COMES OUT HERE AND GETS HIMSELF A CHEAP JOB. SOMEBODY SPOTS HIM, AND THE MOB DECIDES TO TAKE A LITTLE REVENGE...

THEY CALL A COUPLE OF GUYS TO PENCIL IKKY ROSSEN. BUT THE MOB DECIDES IT WOULD BE KIND OF CUTE TO FRAME A GUY THEY ALREADY DON'T LIKE, FOR FINGERING A HOOD NAMED LARSEN. "LOOK, WE EVEN GOT TIME TO PLAY FOOTSIE WITH A PRIVATE EYE." SO THEY SEND A RINGER.

THE TORRENCE BROTHERS AIN'T RINGERS. THEY'RE REAL HARD BOYS. THEY PROVED IT -- EVEN IF THEY DID MAKE A MISTAKE.

MISTAKE NOTHING. THEY GOT IKKY ROSSEN. YOU'RE JUST A SINGING COMMERCIAL IN THIS DEAL, AND AS OF NOW YOU'RE UNDER ARREST FOR MURDER.

GOODBYE, MARLOWE.

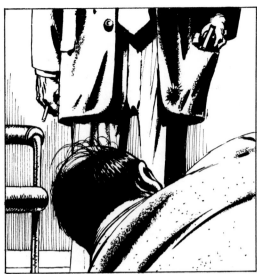

THE OUTFIT WILL GET YOU OUT OF THE CLINK AND BLOW YOU DOWN. YOU SERVED YOUR PURPOSE AND YOU FAILED TO FINGER ME INTO A PATSY.

WHAT ARE YOU TRYING TO DO TO ME? I PAID YOU. I PAID YOU DAMN WELL.

I LOVE YOU, MARLOWE. YOU'RE A REAL PAL.

WHAT I CAN'T SEE IS WHY THEY DRAGGED YOU INTO IT, WHY THEY SET UP THE FAKE IKKY ROSSEN, WHY DIDN'T THEY JUST LET THE TWO LIFE-TAKERS DO THEIR JOB?

I COULDN'T REALLY SAY...UNLESS THIS LARSEN GUY WHO WENT TO THE GAS CHAMBER WAS BIGGER THAN ANYONE THOUGHT, THE MOB MIGHT HAVE HAD MY NAME ON A WAITING LIST.

BUT WHY WAIT? THEY'D GO AFTER YOU QUICKLY?

THEY CAN AFFORD TO WAIT. WHO'S GOING TO BOTHER THEM? EXCEPT WHEN THEY MAKE A MISTAKE.

THE MONEY WORRIES ME. FIVE GRAND OF THEIR DIRTY MONEY. WHAT DO I DO WITH IT?

DON'T BE A JERK ALL YOUR LIFE. YOU EARNED THE MONEY AND YOU RISKED YOUR LIFE FOR IT.

YOU CAN BUY SERIES "E" BONDS--THEY'LL MAKE THE MONEY CLEAN.

MARLOWE, WOULD YOU CONSIDER KISSING A GIRL WITHOUT WEARING YOUR HAT?

SURE.

SERIES "E" BONDS.

TROUBLE IS
MY BUSINESS

Adapted by
JAMES ROSE

Illustrated by
LEE MOYER &
ALFREDO ALCALA

Lettered by
WILLIE SCHUBERT

WHO'S THE GIRL?

HARRIET HUNTRESS-- A SWELL NAME FOR THE PART TOO. SHE LIVES AT THE EL MILANO, VERY HIGH-CLASS.

HER FATHER WENT BROKE IN THIRTY-ONE AND JUMPED OUT HIS OFFICE WINDOW. MOTHER DEAD. KID SISTER IN BOARDING SCHOOL.

WHO DUG UP ALL THIS?

THE CLIENT GOT A BUNCH OF NOTES THE PUP HAD GIVEN TO MARTY. FIFTY GRAND WORTH.

THE PUP DENIED THE NOTES, SO THE CLIENT HAD THE NOTES EXPERTED BY A GUY NAMED ARBOGAST.

BUT HE'S TOO FAT TO DO LEGWORK, AND HE'S OFF THE CASE NOW.

THIS CLIENT--DOES HE HAVE A NAME?

SON, YOU HAVE A TREAT COMING. HAVE MISTER JEETER COME IN, HONEY.

MY TIME HAPPENS TO BE VALUABLE, *MISS HALSEY.*

MR. JEETER, YOU WANTED TO SEE THE OPERATIVE I SELECTED.

I WAS THINKING MORE OF A GENTLEMAN.

YOU'RE NOT THE JEETER OF *TOBACCO ROAD,* ARE YOU?

YOU INSULT ME, ME--A MAN IN MY POSITION.

NOW WAIT A MINUTE.

WAIT A MINUTE NOTHING! THIS PARTY SAID I WASN'T A GENTLEMAN.

A MAN IN *MY* POSITION DOESN'T TAKE A DIRTY CRACK FROM ANYBODY.

I APOLOGIZE, YOUNG MAN. I HAD NO DESIRE TO BE RUDE.

I KNEW YOU WEREN'T THE JEETER OF *TOBACCO ROAD* ALL ALONG.

ARE YOU WILLING TO GIVE THIS HUNTRESS GIRL A LITTLE MONEY--FOR EXPENSES?

4

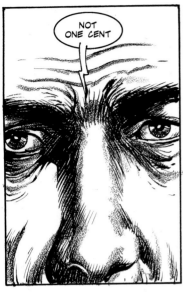

NOT ONE CENT

SUPPOSE SHE MARRIED HIM. WHAT WOULD HE HAVE?

AT THE MOMENT, A THOUSAND DOLLARS A MONTH.

WHEN HE IS TWENTY-EIGHT YEARS OLD, FAR TOO MUCH MONEY.

HOW ABOUT MARTY ESTEL? ANYTHING THERE?

UN-COLLECTIBLE. IT'S A GAMBLING DEBT.

IF YOUR SON HAD WON, MARTY WOULD HAVE PAID HIM.

I'M NOT INTERESTED IN THAT.

YEAH, BUT THINK OF MARTY. HOW WILL HE SLEEP AT NIGHT?

YOU MEAN THERE IS DANGER OF VIOLENCE?

IT'S HARD TO SAY. THINGS CAN HAPPEN--A LONG WAY OFF FROM WHERE MARTY IS.

I PAY FOR RESULTS. I THINK W UNDERSTAND ONE ANOTHER.

The Arbogast I wanted was John D. Arbogast and he had an office on Sunset near Ivar.

SUNSET

SUNSET GRILLE

JOHN D. ARBOGAST, EXAMINER OF QUESTIONED DOCUMENTS

PRIVATE INVESTIGATOR

BZZZZZT

I went over and listened--no sound inside.

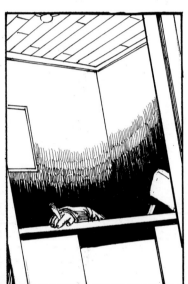

He was fat all right, enormously fat, fatter by far than Anna Halsey.

The paper was from a scratch pad. It would be very nice if it had a message on it.

He had tried to write something after he was shot but all he managed was some hen scratches.

I wiped doorknobs with my handkerchief, and put out the lights in the anteroom.

I left the building and left the neighborhood.

So far as I could tell nobody saw me go.

So far as I could tell.

The El Milano was in the 1900 block on North Sycamore. It was most of the block.

I'VE GOT A CAR OUTSIDE THAT NEEDS 'BOUT FIVE BUCKS WORTH OF DUSTING.

WOULD ANYTHING ELSE BE INCLUDED?

A LITTLE. IS MISS HUNTRESS' CAR IN?

YES, SIR. IT IS IN.

I SUGGEST THAT YOU SAVE YOUR FIVE DOLLARS, AND TRY THE CUSTOMARY MODE OF ENTRY.

8

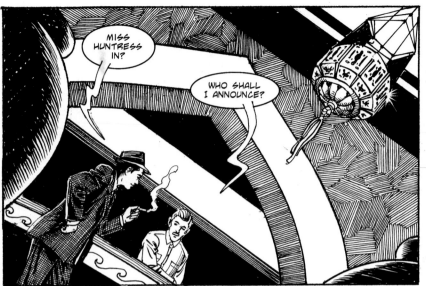

I'M NICE PEOPLE, BUT I GOTTA PROTECT THE GUESTS.

YOU'RE ALMOST OUT OF CIGARS.

MISS HUNTRESS? THERE'S A GENTLEMAN IN MY OFFICE WANTING TO SEE YOU WITH A MESSAGE FROM MARTY ESTEL.

WELL, WHAT'S THE MESSAGE, BROWN-EYES?

I'D HAVE TO COME IN. I NEVER COULD TALK ON MY FEET.

YOU'D BETTER HAVE A DRINK. YOU PROBABLY CAN'T TALK WITHOUT A GLASS IN YOUR HAND.

SO YOU'RE FROM MARTY ESTEL.

NEVER MET HIM.

MARTY WILL LOVE TO HEAR HOW YOU USED HIS NAME.

10.

YOU AMUSE ME. I SHOULD TELL YOU TO GO TO HELL, BUT I LIKE BROWN EYES.

MY FAMILY WERE NICE PEOPLE. OLD MAN JEETER RUINED MY FATHER.

HE *RUINED* HIM. MY FATHER COMMITTED SUICIDE, AND MY MOTHER DIED.

I'VE GOT A KID SISTER BACK EAST IN SCHOOL AND PERHAPS I'M NOT TOO DAMN PARTICULAR HOW I GET THE MONEY.

AND MAYBE I'M GOING TO TAKE CARE OF OLD JEETER ONE OF THESE DAYS, TOO.

RUIN HIM, BABY. I LOVE TO SEE THESE HARD NUMBERS BEND AT THE KNEES.

Falling, I had hit my head on the leg of a chair.

That had hurt me a lot more than young Jeeter's haymaker.

The room was empty. It was full of silence and the memory of a nice perfume.

Hawkins smiled at me. I smiled back. Everything was swell.

It was a lovely night. Venus in the west was as bright as Miss Huntress' eyes.

I crashed five red lights on the way back but my luck was in and nobody pinched me.

I got the key into my door, unlocked it and stepped inside.

I was a world-beater. I took them in sets, guns and all.

The tall man stood and leered and didn't shoot.

14

WE DON'T MEAN NO HARM. NOT THIS TRIP.

MAYBE YOU'RE A GUY THAT'LL TAKE A HINT. LAY OFF THE JEETER KID, THAT'S THE WORD, SEE?

GIMME MY GAT.

LAY OFF, DUMMY. WE JUST GOT A MESSAGE FOR GUY. WE DON'T BLAST HIM.

NOW YOU'RE LOOKING AT A LUGER. WHO'S THE JEETER KID?

MISTER, I PACK THIS SMALL-BORE BECAUSE I CAN SHOOT.

IF YOU THINK YOU CAN TAKE ME, GO AHEAD.

O.K. DO YOU KNOW ANYBODY NAMED ARBOGAST?

MAYBE YES, MAYBE NO. SO LONG, PAL. BE CAREFUL.

let him go. He didn't look like a killer to me, but I could have been wrong.

RRRINGG RRRING

I had dozed off in the chair, which was a bad mistake.

MR. MARLOWE? THIS IS MR. JEETER.

I BELIEVE WE MET THIS MORNING. I'M AFRAID I WAS A LITTLE *STIFF* WITH YOU.

I'M A LITTLE STIFF MYSELF. YOUR SON POKED ME IN THE JAW.

I MEAN YOUR STEPSON, OR YOUR ADOPTED SON-- OR WHATEVER HE IS.

16

HE IS BOTH MY STEPSON AND MY ADOPTED SON.

SHE LIKED HIM POKING ME IN THE JAW.

I HAVE BEEN THINKING THAT PERHAPS SOME CONSIDERATION--NOT LARGE, OF COURSE--SHOULD BE GRANTED TO HER.

FIFTY GRAND IS THE PRICE. I OFFERED HER FIVE HUNDRED--JUST FOR A GAG.

YOU SEEM TO TREAT THIS WHOLE BUSINESS WITH CONSIDERABLE LEVITY.

A COUPLE OF GUNMEN JUST STRUCK ME UP IN MY APARTMENT HERE AND I DON'T SEE WHY IT SHOULD GET SO TOUGH.

GOOD HEAVENS! I'M SENDING MY CAR AND CHAUFFEUR. HIS NAME IS GEORGE.

The car was there already.

I could see it half a block down the side street.

A man stepped out of the shadows, tossing a cigarette over his shoulder.

MISTER MARLOWE?

YEAH. AT EASE. DON'T TELL ME THAT'S OLD MAN JEETER'S CAR.

ONE OF THEM.

18

We went west, through the heart of Hollywood, down the Strip.

To the cool quiet of Beverly Hills where the bridle path divides the bouldevard.

We gave Beverly Hills the swift and swung north into Bel-Air.

Nothing stirred. There was no sound but the soft purr of the tires on concrete.

102 CALVELLO

We swung left again and I caught a sign which read Calvello Drive.

DAMN DRUNK.

HONK!

RRRROAR!

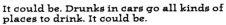

It could be. Drunks in cars go all kinds of places to drink. It could be.

REACH, YOU BASTARDS!

dropped--fast. The gun in his hand belched flame. Somebody must have put a firing pin in it.

I MUST SAY YOU TAKE YOUR TIME ABOUT OBEYING ORDERS.

LISTEN, MR. JEETER, I'VE HAD A HARD DAY. YOUR SON PUNCHED ME IN THE JAW. I FELL. CUT MY HEAD OPEN.

WHEN I STAGGERED BACK TO MY APARTMENT I WAS STUCK UP BY A COUPLE OF HARD GUYS WHO TOLD ME TO LAY OFF THE JEETER CASE.

YOU WANT TO CALL ALL THE PLAYS IN THIS GAME, YOU CAN CARRY THE BALL YOURSELF.

ANY COPS VISIT YOU TONIGHT?

COPS? WHAT FOR?

THERE WAS A STIFF IN FRONT OF YOUR GATES HALF AN HOUR AGO.

ARE YOU SERIOUS?

WHAT'S MORE. HE TOOK A SHOT AT GEORGE AND ME.

YOU COME OUT HERE AT ONCE! AT ONCE, DO YOU HEAR ME?

GEORGE WILL TELL YOU.

OKAY, PAL. MAYBE SOME DAY I CAN PUT YOU ON A SOFT JOB.

Something was bothering me.

I had a feeling it was going to bother me a lot more before I was through.

24

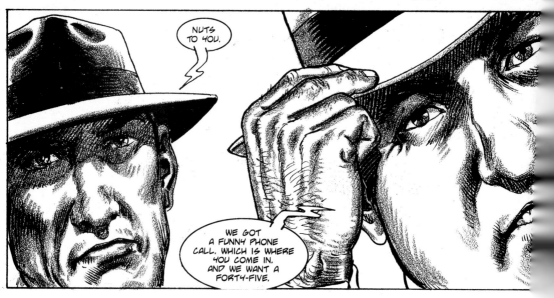

I NEVER HAD A FORTY-FIVE. A GUY WHO NEEDS THAT MUCH GUN OUGHT TO USE A PICK.

NO IDEAS AT ALL, HUH?

JUST FOR WISECRACKS.

WELL, WE GOTTA LOOK AROUND.

MAYBE WE SHOULD HAVE BROUGHT A SEARCH WARRANT.

I DON'T *HAVE* TO FIGHT THIS GUY, DO I?

HIS WIFE LEFT HIM DAY BEFORE YESTERDAY. HE'S JUST TRYING TO COMPENSATE, AS THE FELLOW SAYS.

I GOT ANOTHER KILLING, TOO. A GUY IN YOUR RACKET, MARLOWE.

A FAT GUY ON SUNSET. NAME OF ARBOGAST. EVER HEAR OF HIM?

I THOUGHT HE WAS A HANDWRITING EXPERT.

ARBOGAST WAS SHOT THREE TIMES WITH A TARGET PISTOL.

COME ON, BEN.

I waited fifteen minutes before I went out again.

I drove towards the El Milano.

The lobby hadn't changed any.

JUST THE GUY I WAS HOPING TO SEE. LET'S US GO UPSTAIRS.

NOBODY AIN'T KIDDIN' ANYBODY, I HOPE.

NOW, NOW, GENTS--

WHAT'S THE MATTER, BEEF?

AIN'T NOTHING THE MATTER.

SHOW THE COMPANY IN, BEEF.

LIFT THE DOGS.

THIS IS THE GUY MR. ESTEL. C IN EARLIER TO AND SAID H WAS FROM YOU.

GI HIM A BE

SCRAM.

HUH?

YOU HEARD HIM. WANT YOUR FANNY OUT THE DOOR FIRST, HUH?

I'VE GOT TO LOOK AFTER MY FRIENDS, DON'T I?

GIVE ME BACK MY GUN AND TELL ME WHAT MAKES MY BUSINESS YOUR BUSINESS.

PLENTY. FIRST OFF, HARRIET'S NOT HOME. I CAN'T WAIT ANYMORE. GOT TO GO TO WORK AT THE CLUB.

SO WHAT DID YOU COME AFTER THIS TIME?

LOOKING FOR THE JEETER BOY. SOMEBODY SHOT AT HIS CAR TONIGHT.

YOU THINK I PLAY GAMES LIKE THAT?

I ASKED YOU A QUESTION.

YOU HOLD FIFTY GRAND OF THE BOY'S PAPER. THAT LOOKS BAD FOR YOU, IF ANYTHING HAPPENS TO THE BOY.

I DON'T FIGURE IT THAT WAY. BECAUSE THAT WAY, I'D LOSE MY DOUGH.

LISTEN, MARLOWE, THERE ARE LOTS OF WAYS TO PLAY ANY GAME. I PLAY MINE ON THE HOUSE PERCENTAGE, BECAUSE THAT'S ALL I NEED TO WIN.

JEETER HIRED A MAN NAMED ARBOGAST TO DO A LITTLE WORK. ARBOGAST WAS KILLED IN HIS OFFICE TODAY--WITH A TWENTY-TWO.

THERE WAS A TAIL ON YOU WHEN YOU WENT THERE-- AND YOU DIDN'T GIVE IT TO THE LAW.

DOES THAT MAKE YOU AND ME FRIENDS?

IT SEEMS IT DOES.

WELL, I'LL BE GOING. GIVE THE GUY BACK HIS LUGER, BEEF.

I noticed something I should have noticed the instant I stepped into the room. and then I noticed something else.

The bed had been moved over until its head overlapped the edge of the closet door.

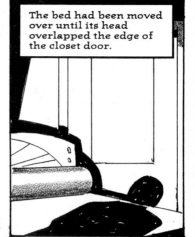

He came out—sideways, in a sort of roll.

He was still big, still blonde, still dressed in rough sporty material.

There was a scorched and soggy stain on the rough coat—about where his heart would be.

Something glittered on the floor. A woman's purse gun.

I put the gun in my pocket.

Hawkins was back again, to see what delayed me.

I DIDN'T SEE YOU LEAVE, SO I CAME UP.

He had a mean look in his eye.

ALL SET, I GUESS SHE WON'T BE HOME FOR A WHILE.

Hawkins saw me out. He saw me downstairs and off the premises.

I got into my car and drove off home.

I rode up in the elevator and unlocked the door and clicked the light on.

Waxnose sat in my best chair.

34

HI, PAL. YOU STILL AIN'T HAD THAT DOOR FIXED. KIND OF SHUT IT, HUH?

I shut the door, stood looking across the room at him.

SO, YOU KILLED MY PAL.

YOU TOLD ME HIS GUN HAD NO FIRING PIN.

YEAH, HE FOOLED ME ON THAT, THE LITTLE SO-AND-SO. HE WAS MY KID BROTHER.

YOU DON'T SEE SO GOOD.

THE CHAUFFEUR GOT HIM WITH A SMITH AND WESSON FORTY-FOUR. I DIDN'T EVEN FIRE.

WHAT DID YOU KILL ARBOGAST FOR? WHAT DID HE EVER DO TO YOUR FILTHY LITTLE BROTHER?

YOU GOT GUTS. I DON'T KNOW ANY ARBOGAST.

I AIN'T KILLED NOBOD[Y] AT ALL, FRIEN[D]. NOBODY.

He came towards me softly across the room.

I GUESS THIS IS YOUR LUCKY DAY. I GOTTA GO A PLACE AND SEE A GUY.

But I had a guy to see too—and I wanted to see him first.

NOT YET.

GREEDY GUY. WHY DID I EVER LEAVE SAINT LOOEY?

I hit him a third time. I never hit anything harder.

I snapped handcuffs on his wrists and pulled him into the dressing room.

I left him, a funny lad, not all bad, but not so pure I had to weep over him either.

I left with my three guns. There was nobody outside the apartment house.

36

The butler opened a wide door and I stepped past him into an oval room with a black and silver rug.

GET OUT AND KEEP THOSE DOORS *SHUT!* I'M NOT HOME TO ANYBODY, UNDERSTAND?

The butler closed the doors. Presumably, he went away. I didn't hear him go.

YOU MADE A NICE COME-BACK.

YOU TOOK A CHANCE LEAVING ME IN YOUR APART-MENT.

I MIGHT HAVE SNEAKED SOME OF YOUR PER-FUME.

A NICE SORT OF DETECTIVE YOU TURNED OUT TO BE.

YOU WALK RIGHT IN ON MISS HUNTRESS AND EXPLAIN THE WHOLE THING TO HER.

IT WORKED, DIDN'T IT?

I KNOW A NICE GIRL WHEN I SEE ONE.

SHE'S HERE TELLING YOU SHE HAD AN IDEA SHE GOT NOT TO LIKE, AND FOR YOU TO QUIT WORRYING ABOUT IT.

I REGARD YOU AS INCOMPETENT. MY SON IS MISSING.

I'M WORKING FOR ANNA HALSEY. ANY COMPLAINTS YOU HAVE TO MAKE SHOULD BE ADDRESSED TO HER.

SHOULD I GIVE HIM THE HEAVE, SIR?

DON'T BE SILLY.

WHAT DO YOU MEAN YOUR SON IS MISSING, MR. JEETER?

WHAT DO YOU SUPPOSE I MEAN?

I SHOULD HAVE THOUGHT THAT WOULD BE CLEAR ENOUGH-- EVEN TO YOU.

NOBODY KNOWS WHERE HE IS.

MISS HUNTRESS DOESN'T KNOW.

I DON'T KNOW.

BUT I KNOW.

38

Nobody moved for a long minute.

MISTER GERALD IS AT THE EL MILANO. HE WENT BACK THERE TO WAIT FOR MISS HUNTRESS.

WELL-- I'M GLAD TO HEAR IT.

It was hard to watch all three of them. But they didn't move.

I WAS AFRAID HE WAS OFF SOMEWHERE GETTING DRUNK.

NO. HE'S NOT OFF ANYWHERE GETTING DRUNK.

LET'S GO BACK OVER THIS THING A LITTLE. WE'RE ALL WISE TO THE SITUATION. I KNOW GEORGE IS.

THIS ARBOGAST...WHEN I WENT TO SEE HIM, HE WAS DEAD--SHOT THREE TIMES.

NO, I DIDN'T TELL THE POLICE, MR. JEETER.

SOMEBODY RUBBED HIM OUT THIS AFTERNOON WITH A TWENTY-TWO.

A DIMWIT CALLED FRISKY LAVON WAS SHOT DEAD IN FRONT OF YOUR HOUSE TONIGHT. THAT'S TWO.

WE NOW COME TO THE THIRD AND MOST IMPORTANT.

BACK AT THE EL MILANO I FOUND THAT HAWKINS HAD LET MARTY ESTEL AND HIS BODYGUARD INTO MISS HUNTRESS' APARTMENT.

HE WENT AWAY AND I POKED AROUND. AND I FOUND YOUNG GERALD IN THE BEDROOM, IN A CLOSET.

EVER SEE THIS BEFORE?

YES, IT'S MINE.

I DON'T KNOW MUCH ABOUT GUNS. I TOOK IT OUT TO SHOW SOMEBODY--IT WAS GEORGE I SHOWED IT TO.

HE'S DEAD, OF COURSE. SHOT THROUGH THE HEART-- PROBABLY WITH THIS GUN. IT WAS LEFT THERE WITH HIM.

YOU DAMNED MURDERESS!

CLICK

IT'S *OBVIOUS* WHO KILLED HIM, MISS HUNTRESS.

IT'S SIMPLY A MATTER OF MOTIVE AND OPPORTUNITY.

GERALD HAD FIVE MILLION COMING TO HIM IN TWO YEARS. IF HE DIED, WHO'S HIS NATURAL HEIR?

DID YOU KNOW THAT IN THE STATE OF CALIFORNIA A MAN CAN, BY HIS OWN ACT, BECOME A NATURAL HEIR?

JUST BY ADOPTING SOMEBODY WHO HAS MONEY AND NO HEIRS!

George moved then. His movement was as smooth as a ripple of water.

She didn't know very much about guns.

CRAK!

GEORGE WOULD BACK GERALD INTO THE CLOSET, AND THERE, QUIETLY, CALMLY...

...HE WOULD KILL HIM AND DROP THE GUN.

GEORGE KILLED ARBOGAST, TOO. GEORGE LIKES TO KILL PEOPLE. HE MADE A NEAT SHOT AT FRISKY.

MY GOD! MY GOD!

YOU DON'T HAVE ONE--EXCEPT MONEY.

PUT 'EM UP, BUD.

GO AWAY, YOU'RE INTRUDING.

CRAK!

He ran. We heard his footsteps.

GO CALL THE LAW, ANGEL. I'LL WATCH THEM NOW.

ALL RIGHT.

BUT YOU CERTAINLY NEED A LOT OF HELP IN YOUR BUSINESS, MR. MARLOWE.

I had been in there for a solid hour, alone.

GUYS LIKE YOU GET IN A LOT OF TROUBLE.

CENTRAL HOMICIDE

TROUBLE IS MY BUSINESS.

SIGN THREE COPIES.

CENTRAL HOMICIDE

42

started to say and stopped. I was tired of that gag for that night.

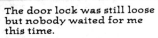

The door lock was still loose but nobody waited for me this time.

MARLOWE

The *noir* detective story has been parodied, plundered and imitated so much over the years that it has come to be regarded as a contrived and simplistic genre. But in this age where the distance between the "haves" and the "have-nots" is greater than ever, the *noir* genre takes on new relevance and meaning.

The works of Chandler, Cain, Hammett and Conrad are anything but simplistic. Certainly they are works of fantasy. The plots are darkly byzantine, the characters morally disenfranchised. We witness the events of a hostile, corrupt world through their keen eyes and quiet voices in detached fashion.

Philip Marlowe is perhaps one of the most contradictory yet believable characters inhabiting this world. He is taciturn yet glib. Honest yet conniving. Misogynistic yet romantic. Somehow, these qualities not only co-existed in the same character, but seemed strangely compatible. He was often victim, and master of the same situation, as are we all. He was cheated, manipulated, deceived and abused in his quest for the truth. Not a grand heroic quest, mind you. But a job, for $25 a day plus expenses. Perhaps that is why he is believable. He represents the basic conflict of the human condition.

Chandler wrote that ". . . the detective exists complete and entire and unchanged by anything that happens, that he is, as detective, outside the story, and above it, and always will be." And yet, Marlowe is inexorably drawn into the machinations of those around him. Often the final solution means sacrifice. To Marlowe, that is just another part of the job.

Chandler described Marlowe in grim terms: "His moral and intellectual force is that he gets nothing but his fee, for which he will, if he can, protect the innocent, guard the helpless and destroy the wicked, and the fact that he must do this while earning out a meager living is what makes him stand out."

In this series of stories, we not only present Chandler's characters to a new generation, but to a new medium as well. There have been several portrayals of Marlowe in films over the years: Bogart, Powell, Mitchum, and others. And now we'll see some new interpretations of him. Each stylistically different, but all unmistakably Marlowe.

Dean Motter

RAYMOND CHANDLER,

one of the twentieth century's most admired authors, was born in Chicago in 1888 and educated at Dulwich College, England. He worked at various times as poet, teacher, book reviewer, and accountant. During World War I he served in Britain's Royal Air Force. In 1919 he returned to the United States where he became director for a number of independent oil companies. After the Great Depression of the 1930s put an end to his business, he turned to writing. The first of his stories appeared in *Black Mask* magazine. His first Philip Marlowe novel, *The Big Sleep,* was published in 1939. It was followed by *Farewell, My Lovely; The High Window; The Lady in the Lake; The Little Sister; The Long Goodbye;* and *Playback.* Chandler lived for many years in Southern California. He passed away in 1959.